KU-587-332

LUCAN
LIBRARY
TEL. 6216422

Beng Ling

Beng Ling Neoh aka Beng Ling Johnson has been a Visiting Teacher for Deaf and Hard of Hearing Children in Ireland since 2006. She started her vocation in Federation School for the Deaf, Penang, Malaysia in 1985. Her interest in learning more about deaf education, especially inclusion in mainstream setting, brought her to Manchester University to pursue MEd in Education for Hearing Impaired Children (International) in 1997.

Colin

Colin Johnson is a writer and occupational therapist from County Kildare. He has learned a lot about the needs of deaf and hard of hearing children from Beng Ling Neoh.

Callum

Callum Knight is an illustrator currently studying at the National College of Art and Design, Dublin.

For all deaf or hard of hearing children

who work hard in school

and their caring teachers.

Copyright © Beng Ling Neoh & Colin Johnson, 2017
First Published in Ireland, in 2017, in co-operation with
Choice Publishing, Drogheda, County Louth,
Republic of Ireland.
www.choicepublishing.ie

Paperback ISBN: 978-1-911131-28-1

All rights reserved. No part of this publication may be reproduced, stored in a retrieval system, transmitted in any form, or by any means, electronic, mechanical, photocopying, recording or otherwise, without the prior permission of the copyright holder.

Illustrator: Callum Knight ©

A CIP catalogue record for this book is available from
the National Library.

Lucky Lucy Logan

Written by: Beng Ling Neoh and Colin Johnson

Illustrated by: Callum Knight

Lucy Logan is a lucky girl.

She's always been lucky.

Like the time she fell off her bike ... and landed in a bed of strawberries.

Or the time she missed school because she had a cough ... the same day the toilets flooded the classroom!

Lucky Lucy Logan!

One day the teacher noticed Lucy couldn't hear very well, especially when it was noisy or when she couldn't see the teacher. Sometimes she missed what the teacher said and in big groups, she couldn't keep up.

Luckily she got new hearing aids AND an FM System. Now the teacher wears a microphone and her voice comes through the hearing aids, straight into Lucy's ears.

So now, Lucy can hear the teacher all the time, even when she isn't close by.

When it's noisy she still needs to see the teacher's face, but it's much better than before.

Lucky Lucy Logan!

Lucy

Miss Nolan

Noreen Nolan is Lucy's teacher.

Noreen Nolan is not so lucky.

When she fell off her bike, she landed in nettles.

The day the toilet flooded, she was wearing sandals.

Not-so-lucky Miss Nolan!

Today, Miss Nolan is reading a story to the class.

Miss Nolan is a great reader – the class loves to listen to her stories and often join in. It can be quite noisy.

Miss Nolan is holding the book close to her face. It's hard for Lucy to tell what Miss Nolan is saying when her face is hidden.

When Miss Nolan finishes the chapter, she snaps the book shut ... on her nose!

She shrieks and drops the book. Now Lucy can see her face.

Lucky Lucy Logan!

Not-so-lucky Miss Nolan!

Miss Nolan decides to walk around the room while she talks to the class.

Lucy can't see her teacher's face again and she can't tell what Miss Nolan is saying.

Miss Nolan catches her foot on Britney Barry's bag ... and falls flat on her face!

She decides not to walk around any more.

Lucky Lucy Logan!

Not-so-lucky Miss Nolan!

Miss Nolan sits on the radiator by the window.

It's a bright day outside which means that Miss Nolan is in dark shadow and Lucy can't see her face.

But the radiator is HOT and Miss Nolan jumps up screaming and holding her bum ... and moves away from the window.

Lucky Lucy Logan!

Not-so-lucky Miss Nolan!

Miss Nolan opens the window because it is hot. Another class is playing outside and having fun.

But Lucy's hearing aids make the outside noise really loud and she can't hear Miss Nolan properly.

A magpie flies in through the window and lands in Miss Nolan's hair. Miss Nolan closes the window.

Lucky Lucy Logan!

Not-so-lucky Miss Nolan!

Miss Nolan loves necklaces. Today she is wearing her favourite one. A big shiny disc.

It keeps banging against the microphone - this means that Lucy hears a loud clanging noise and it hurts her ears.

But magpies love shiny things as well. The magpie in Miss Nolan's hair steals the necklace ... and nearly strangles Miss Nolan as it flies away.

Now Miss Nolan has no necklace.

Lucky Lucy Logan!

Not-so-lucky Miss Nolan!

Miss Nolan really likes Mr Parsons, the Principal.

Mr Parsons comes to the class and asks to speak to Miss Nolan. Miss Nolan goes outside ... but she forgets to mute her microphone, so Lucy can still hear her through her FM System.

"Sorry to interrupt", says Mr Parsons, "But this can't wait. I've fancied you for ages. Will you go out with me, Noreen Nolan?"

Miss Nolan gasps.

Lucy gasps ... then she giggles and whispers the news to her friends. Her friends are amazed!

Lucky Lucy Logan!

Lucky Noreen Nolan!

Hints for teachers using FM System (or similar):

Allow the child a clear view of your face. While speaking to the class, avoid:

    covering your face

    looking away or walking around

    standing by windows (your face may be in shadow)

Remember the microphone signal transmits directly to the child's hearing aid(s). Avoid:

    wearing jewellery or scarves that may clank or rustle
        against the microphone

    standing next to anything producing noise, e.g. projector,
        open window

At the start of the day/lesson, discreetly check with the child that the system is working.

Remember to use 'mute' function when working 1:1 with another child or ~~flirting with~~ speaking to a colleague.

LUCAN
LIBRARY
TEL. 6216422